D.W. ALL WET

LITTLE, BROWN AND COMPANY

New York ~ Boston

For Brenda Gardner,
with warm scones and hot tea

Little, Brown and Company

Hachette Book Group USA
237 Park Avenue, New York, NY 10017
Visit our Web site at www.lb-kids.com

First Paperback Edition: April 1991

D.W.™ is a trademark of Marc Brown.
ISBN 978-0-316-11268-0

Library of Congress Catalog Card Number 87-15752
Library of Congress Cataloging-in-Publication information is available.

PB: 20 19 18 17 16 15 14 13 12
SC
Manufactured in China

"It's too hot!" shouted D.W.

"That's why we came to the beach," said Mother.

"I don't like the beach," said D.W.

"And I don't like to get wet."

"Here's a good spot," said Father.
"When are we leaving?" asked D.W.
"We just got here," said Mother.

"Come on, D.W. Take off your robe," said Arthur.
"Last one in is a rotten egg!"

"I'm not playing," said D.W.
"I don't want to get sunburned.
And no splashing!"

"Come on in," called Arthur. "The water's great!"
"I don't want to," said D.W. "I don't like the water."

"You haven't even tried it,"
said Father.

"Is it time to go yet?" asked D.W.
"Not yet," said Arthur.
"I'm going for a walk."

"Me, too!" said D.W.
"You walk. I'll ride.

"Help me up!"

"But I can't see!" said Arthur.
"You don't need to," said D.W.
"I'll tell you where to go.

"Go!" she said.
"Where are we going?" asked Arthur.

"It's a surprise," said D.W. "Keep walking.
Now turn left."

"Arthur, I said *left*. Turn *left!*" cried D.W.

"Not that way! Stop!"

SPLASH!

"Help! Help!" screamed D.W. "I can't swim!"

"You don't have to," said Arthur. "Just stand up."

Then D.W. dipped,

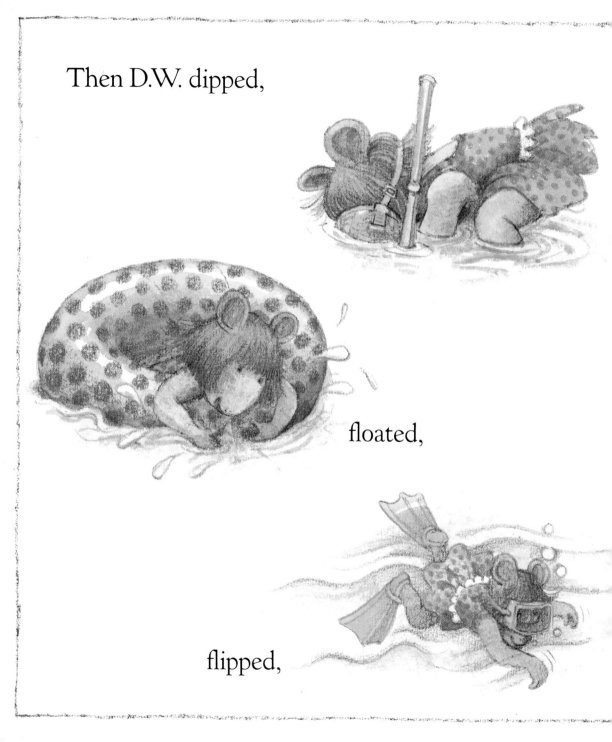

floated,

flipped,

flopped,

squirted,

splashed,

and dunked.

"Time to go!" called Father.

"Let's come back tomorrow!" said D.W.